LAUGH
-Out-
LOUD
SPOOKY
JOKES
for KIDS

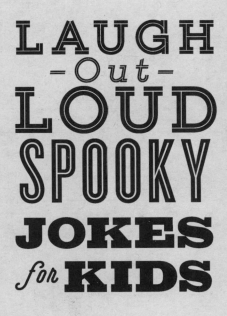

LAUGH
-Out-
LOUD
SPOOKY
JOKES
for KIDS

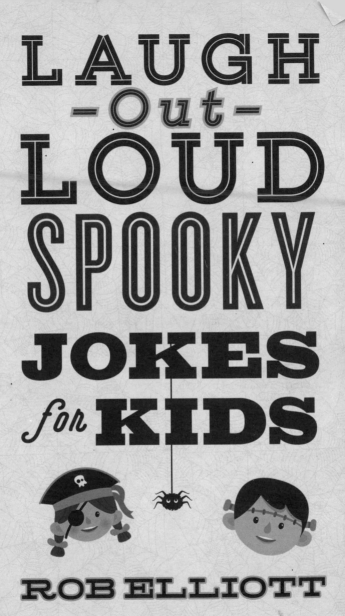

ROB ELLIOTT

HARPER

An Imprint of HarperCollins Publishers

Library of Congress Control Number: 2016941667
ISBN 978-0-06-249788-8

Typography by Gearbox
16 17 18 19 20   PC/BRR   10 9 8 7 6 5 4 3
❖
First Edition

To every foster child served by the dedicated staff of Lutheran Social Services of Michigan. You inspire us all with your courage, hope, and laughter.

Q: What kind of music do mummies like to listen to?

A: Wrap music

Q: Why did Dracula go to the doctor?

A: Because he couldn't stop coffin.

Q: Why do ghosts make horrible fans?

A: Because they're always booing!

Q: What monster is the best at hide-and-seek?

A: A where-wolf

Q: Who is the smartest monster of all?

A: Frank-Einstein

Q: Why did the ghost need a tissue?

A: Because he had a lot of boo-gers.

Q: What kind of bug will never die?

A: A zom-bee

Q: Who was the most famous painter of monsters?

A: Vincent van Ghost

Q: How can you tell when a mummy is stressed out?

A: It gets unraveled.

- -

Q: What is a spider's favorite workout?

A: A spin class

Q: Why can't you ever tell a skeleton a secret?

A: Because it just goes in one ear and out the
other.

Q: Why didn't the skeleton cross the road?

A: He didn't have the guts.

Q: What's a witch's favorite subject?

A: Spell-ing

**Q: What do you get when you
mix a vampire and a baseball?**

A: A baseball bat

- -

Q: What kind of monster lives in a tissue?

A: The boogey-man

Q: What do you call a pretty ghost?

A: Boo-tiful

Q: What kind of dog does Dracula own?

A: A bloodhound

Q: What kind of bird is the spookiest?

A: The scarec

Q: What do you call a field full of eyeballs?

A: An eye ch

Q: What kind of eggs do monsters eat?

A: Deviled eggs

Q: What happened to the monster when he ate his vegetables and got lots of sleep?

A: He grew-some.

Q: What does a vampire eat for dinner?

A: Mashed potatoes and grave-y

Q: What does a skeleton we for Halloween?

A: A cos-tomb

- - - - - - - - - - - - - - - - - -

Q: What do you get when a monster goes to the bathroom?

A: Cree-pee

Q: Which monster is the heaviest?

A: A skele-ton

Q: What is a monster's favorite dessert?

A: Ice scream

Q: What did one casket say to the other casket?

A: "Is that you coffin?"

Q: What do monsters put in their chili?

A: Human bean-ings

Q: What do canaries say on Halloween?

A: "Trick or tweet"

Q: Which room is missing in a ghost's house?

A: The living room

Q: How do you watch a scary movie on Halloween?

A: On your flat-scream TV

Q: What do you call an undercover bug?

A: A spy-der

- -

Knock, knock.

Who's there?

Autumn.

Autumn who?

We autumn make some pumpkin pie.

Tongue Twisters—Say each one ten times fast!

Black cats.

Ghosts glow.

Pumpkin pie, please.

Plump pumpkins.

Knock, knock.

Who's there?

Leaf.

Leaf who?

Leaf me some of your Halloween candy.

Q: What is a monster's favorite book?

A: *Little House on the Scary*

Q: Why were the monster's pants too short?

A: Because he grew-some.

Q: What kind of monster do you see on the dance floor?

A: A boogie-man

Q: What do you get when you cross a ghoul and a turkey?

A: A gobble-in

– –

Q: What is a ghost's favorite treat?

A: Boo-berry pie

Q: What does a skeleton say when it goes on a cruise?

A: "Bone voyage."

Q: How do monsters style their hair?

A: With scare spray

Q: Where do ghosts go for spring break?

A: Mali-boo

Q: Why does Dracula have a hard time finding a job?

A: Because he's a pain in the neck.

Q: What is a goblin's favorite ride at the amusement park?

A: The roller ghost-er

Q: How does a ghost unlock its door?

A: With a spoo-key

Q: What kind of ghost always comes back to you?

A: A boo-merang

Knock, knock.

Who's there?

The interrupting ghost.

The inter—

Booooo!

Q: What do werewolves put on their waffles?

A: Whipped scream

Q: What did the mother ghost say to her son when he left for summer camp?

A: "You'll be mist."

Q: What did the witch get at the hotel?

A: Broom service

Q: Why wouldn't the zombie get a job?

A: Because he was a dead-beat!

Q: What instrument does a skeleton play?

A: The trom-bone

Q: Why was the pumpkin afraid to

cross the road?

A: It didn't want to get squash-ed.

Q: What did the boy pumpkin say

to the girl pumpkin?

A: "You're gourd-geous."

Q: How does a monster like his coffee?

A: With scream and sugar

- -

Q: Why did Dracula die at the restaurant?

A: He ordered the chicken-fried stake!

Q: Where do zombies buy their snacks?

A: At the gross-ery store

Q: Why are skeletons lonely on Valentine's Day?

A: Because they don't have a heart.

Knock, knock.

Who's there?

Justin.

Justin who?

You're Justin time to go trick-or-treating

with me.

Q: What does a ghost wear to the beach?

A: A boo-kini

Q: How do monsters protect their skin at the beach?

A: Sun scream

Q: What do you play with a baby ghost?

A: Peeka-boo

Q: Why do mummies eat pickles?

A: So there's never a dill moment.

Q: **What do witches order at the coffee shop?**

A: Hocus mochas

Q: **What do scarecrows wear to parties?**

A: Har-vests

Knock, knock.

Who's there?

Yam.

Yam who?

I yam going to the Halloween party. Are you?

Q: **What did the squash say to the**

jack-o-lantern?

A: "I yam your best friend."

Knock, knock.

Who's there?

Skeleton.

Skeleton who?

No-body is here right now!

Q: What is the best way to find out about spooky spiders?

A: On a web-site

Q: What do wizards eat for lunch?

A: Sand-witches

Q: What do mummies drink?

A: Ghoul-Aid

Knock, knock.

Who's there?

Dishes.

Dishes who?

Dishes the best these Halloween jokes are going to get.

Q: Who did the ghost take to the party?

A: His ghoul-friend

Q: What did the skeleton say to the invisible man?

A: "Long time no see."

Knock, knock.

Who's there?

Irish.

Irish who?

Irish you a Happy Halloween!

Q: Where does Dracula keep his money?

A: In the blood bank

Q: What do you get when you cross a werewolf and an owl?

A: A hoooooowl

Q: What is a math teacher's favorite dessert?

A: Pumpkin pi

Q: Where do skeletons live?

A: On dead-end streets

Q: What do ghosts eat for lunch?

A: Ham-boo-gers and french fries

Q: Why was the pumpkin depressed?

A: It felt all hollow inside.

Q: What game do monsters like to play?

A: Hide-and-shriek

Knock, knock.

Who's there?

Wanda.

Wanda who?

I Wanda suck your blood. . . .

Mwa-hahahaha . . .

Q: What do you get when you combine a ghost and a chicken?

A: A poultry-geist

Q: Where do ghosts like to go swimming?

A: In the Dead Sea

Q: Why did the mummy go on vacation?

A: Because he was all wound up.

Q: What happens when you get kissed by a vampire?

A: Well, I hear it's a pain in the neck!

Q: Why are ghosts such bad liars?

A: Because you can see right through them!

Q: What do you get when you cross Dracula and a snowman?

A: Frostbite

Q: What is a monster's motto?

A: "Eat, drink, and be scary."

Q: How did Dracula fall in love with his girlfriend?

A: All she had to do was bat her eyes.

Q: What do sea monsters eat for dinner?

A: Fish and ships

Q: What do goblins wear trick-or-treating?

A: Cos-tombs

Q: What do you call a werewolf with a camera?

A: A paw-parazzo

Q: How do wizards turn on lights?

A: With light s-witches

Q: What did the baby monster say to its dad?

A: "Where is mummy?"

Q: How do you decide which pie to make for Thanksgiving?

A: You weigh the pros and pe-cons.

Q: What do you call a skeleton that won't work?

A: Lazy-bones

Q: Which monster do you see during the holidays?

A: Santa Claws

- -

Q: What did the boy ghost say to the girl ghost?

A: "You look boo-tiful tonight."

Q: What do you get if you give a black cat a lemon?

A: A sour puss

Q: What does a baby ghost like to wear?

A: Boo-ties

Q: What do you call it when monsters go to dinner and a movie?

A: Intimi-dating

- -

Q: Why are monsters messy eaters?

A: Because they're always goblin.

Q: Why was the vampire a sad vegetarian?

A: Because you can't get blood out of a turnip.

Q: What do you get if you have 3.14 pumpkins?

A: Pumpkin pi

Q: Why did the monster need dental floss?

A: He had someone stuck in his teeth.

Q: What is Frankenstein's favorite food at a cookout?

A: Hallo-weenies

Knock, knock.

Who's there?

Ben.

Ben who?

Ben wanting to go trick-or-treating for a while now.

Q: Why is Dracula so easy to trick on Halloween?

A: Because he's a sucker.

Q: What do you call two tarantulas when they get married?

A: Newly-webs

Knock, knock.

Who's there?

Shellfish.

Shellfish who?

Don't be shellfish with your Halloween candy.

Knock, knock.

Who's there?

Juicy.

Juicy who?

Did juicy my fun Halloween costume?

Q: What does a skeleton say before he sits down to eat?

A: "Bone appetit."

Q: Why did Dracula ask for a piece of gum?

A: Because he had bat breath.

Leah: Why do witches fly on brooms?

Mason: The cord was too short to ride a

vacuum cleaner.

Q: How do ghosts wash their hair?

A: With sham-boo

Knock, knock.

Who's there?

Wanda.

Wanda who?

I Wanda wish you a Happy Halloween.

- -

Q: What kind of cologne do jack-o'-lanterns wear?

A: Pumpkin spice

Q: What kind of pants do ghosts wear?

A: Boo jeans

Knock, knock.

Who's there?

Needle.

Needle who?

I needle little more time to come up with a Halloween costume.

Q: What kind of cars do goblins drive?

A: Monster trucks

- -

Q: What do you call a ghost up your nose?

A: A boo-ger

Q: How do you fix a hole in your pumpkin?

A: With a pumpkin patch

Knock, knock.

Who's there?

Noah.

Noah who?

Noah good place to trick-or-treat around here?

Q: What is a zombie's favorite treat for Halloween?

A: Butter-fingers

Q: What do swamp monsters eat?

A: Marsh-mallows

Q: What happens when you hit a pumpkin with your car?

A: It gets squashed!

Q: What do zombies eat for breakfast?

A: Bacon and legs

Q: What happened when the girl swallowed her apple juice?

A: It was in-cider.

Q: How did Frankenstein feel on vacation?

A: Like he didn't have a scare in the world

Q: What do witches do when they're tired?

A: They sit for a spell.

Q: What is a zombie's favorite kind of cheese?

A: Limb-burger

Q: Who helped the Bride of Frankenstein go to the ball?

A: Her scary godmother

Q: What did one candy apple say to the other?

A: "Let's stick together."

Q: What do you call a dentist who cleans a vampire's teeth?

A: CRAZY!

Q: How did the monster feel when he was struck by lightning?

A: He was shocked!

Josh: Should I tell the police that we saw a mummy?

Jeff: No, I would keep it under wraps!

Q: What is it like to find a skeleton in the freezer?

A: Bone-chilling

Q: What do werewolves think of vampires?

A: They think they're fang-tastic.

Joe: How was the Halloween party?

Sam: It was spook-tacular!

Q: What do you get when you put a pumpkin in a bag?

A: A sack-o-lantern

- -

Q: What's the scariest kind of horse?

A: A night-mare

Q: What do monsters do with their mouthwash?

A: They gargoyle it!

Q: Why was the Creature from the Black Lagoon too busy to go to the Halloween party?

A: He was swamped!

Q: What do you get when you cross a snake and a ghost?

A: A boo-a constrictor

Anna: How much does that tombstone weigh?

Emma: A skele-ton

Q: What kind of boat does Dracula have?

A: A blood vessel

Q: What happens when an ogre eats beans?

A: It's gas-tly.

Q: Why was the gremlin afraid of the goblin's dog?

A: It was pet-rifying.

Q: Who won't drink milk on Halloween?

A: Cow-ards

Q: What is it like to listen to Dracula's heartbeat?

A: Re-pulse-ive

Q: What do you get when you cross a werewolf with a pine tree?

A: A monster whose bark is worse than its bite

Q: What is a vampire's favorite fruit?

A: Neck-tarines

Q: Where do monsters go sailing?

A: On Lake Eerie

Q: What do you call a vampire who's not very smart?

A: A ding-bat

Knock, knock.

Who's there?

Olive.

Olive who?

Olive this Halloween candy is making me sick!

Q: Where did the police put Dracula in the prison?

A: In a blood cell

Knock, knock.

Who's there?

Wheel.

Wheel who?

Wheel have some fun when we go trick-or-treating tonight.

- -

Q: What kind of car does Dracula drive?

A: A bloodmobile

Q: Why do vampires make good artists?

A: Because they like drawing blood.

Q: Why did the scarecrow win the Nobel Prize?

A: Because he was outstanding in his field.

Q: What does Dracula take when he's got a bad cold?

A: Coffin drops

Q: Why did the cyclops stop teaching math?

A: Because he had only one pupil.

Q: What do ghosts eat for supper?

A: S-boo-ghetti

Q: Why didn't the mummy have any friends?

A: He was too wrapped up in himself.

Q: Why couldn't the skeleton stop laughing?

A: Because someone tickled his funny bone.

Q: Why didn't the scarecrow go back for seconds at Thanksgiving dinner?

A: He was already stuffed.

Q: Why don't you want to go into business with a zombie?

A: It will cost you an arm and a leg.

Knock, knock.

Who's there?

Owl.

Owl who?

Happy owl-oween!

Q: Why did the ghost go to the psychiatrist?

A: He felt like a no-body.

Q: What is a scarecrow's favorite kind of fruit?

A: Straw-berries

Q: Why couldn't the jack-o'-lantern scare the trick-or-treaters?

A: It didn't have the guts!

Q: Why did the monster go on a diet?

A: He was having trouble fitting under the kid's bed.

Q: Why are witches good drivers?

A: They know how to drive a stick.

- -

Q: How did the witch know her potion was mixed right?

A: She used spell check.

Q: What's a ghost's favorite kind of sandwich?

A: Boo-logna and cheese

Q: Where do monsters take their toddlers?

A: To day-scare

Q: Why did the monster order chicken for dinner?

A: He was in a fowl mood.

Q: What happened when the skeleton built a snowman?

A: It chilled him to the bone.

Q: What happened when the turkey got in a fight?

A: He got the stuffing knocked out of him.

Q: What happened when the vampire drank old milk?

A: It was blood-curdling!

Q: Why wouldn't the bull go into the haunted house?

A: Because he was a cow-ard.

- -

Q: What's a zombie's favorite kind of tea?

A: Nas-tea!

Q: Why don't vampires wear shoes?

A: Because they have no souls.

Knock, knock.

Who's there?

Sharon.

Sharon who?

I'm Sharon my Halloween candy with you if you open the door!

Q: What does a monster say when he goes trick-or-treating?

A: "Trick or Eat!"

Q: **Where do you go if there is a monster under your bed?**

A: To a hotel for the night

Q: **Why did the vampire join the circus?**

A: He was an acro-bat.

Knock, knock.

Who's there?

Bacon.

Bacon who?

I'm bacon a pumpkin pie. Want some?

- -

Knock, knock.

Who's there?

Funnel.

Funnel who?

The funnel start as soon as you put on your costume!

Knock, knock.

Who's there?

Norway.

Norway who?

There's Norway I'm going to miss Halloween!

Knock, knock.

Who's there?

Count.

Count who?

Count Dracula!

Q: What happened when the duck saw the ghost?

A: He was quacking in his boots!

Q: Why shouldn't you bother a corpse?

A: You might get on their last nerve.

Q: Why did Dracula eat the lightbulb?

A: He wanted a light lunch.

Q: Who helped the pumpkins cross the road?

A: The crossing gourds

- -

Q: Where do zombies like to play?

A: In their graveyard

Knock, knock.

Who's there?

Lego.

Lego who?

Don't Lego of your Halloween candy or

you might lose it.

Q: Why don't you let vampires join the choir?

A: They're always sharp!

Knock, knock.

Who's there?

Phillip.

Phillip who?

Phillip my bag with more candy, please!

Q: **What do you get when you cross a monkey and a vampire?**

A: An orangu-fang

Q: **Why did the mother ghost give her child a time-out?**

A: He just wouldn't boo-have.

Q: **What did one leaf say to the other leaf?**

A: "I think I'm falling for you."

Q: **What is a werewolf's favorite breakfast?**

A: Pigs in a blanket

- -

Q: Why did the turkey cross the road?

A: To prove it wasn't a chicken!

Q: What do ghosts like to put in their cereal?

A: Boo-nanas

Knock, knock.

Who's there?

Pumpkin.

Pumpkin who?

A pumpkin fill up the flat tire on your bike.

Knock, knock.

Who's there?

Butter.

Butter who?

I butter get a bigger bag for all my

Halloween candy!

Q: How did the turkey get across the lake?

A: He used a gravy boat.

Knock, knock.

Who's there?

Howl.

Howl who?

Howl we wait until next year to go trick-or-treating again?

Knock, knock.

Who's there?

Annie.

Annie who?

Annie body want to go with me to get my Halloween costume?

Q: What is a monster's favorite kind of treat?

A: Ghoul Scout cookies

Q: What is the difference between a werewolf and a cow?

A: One howls at the moon, and one jumps over the moooo-n.

Q: What do you call a bird with a high IQ?

A: Owl-bert Einstein

Q: What do scarecrows use to eat?

A: A pitchfork

Q: What skeleton solves mysteries?

A: Sherlock Bones

Knock, knock.

Who's there?

Emma.

Emma who?

Emma little sick from all this Halloween candy.

Q: **What do sea monsters take when they have a cold?**

A: Vitamin sea

Q: **Why did the young spider get grounded?**

A: He was spending too much time on the web.

Q: **Why did Dracula's son wake up in the middle of the night?**

A: He had a bite-mare.

Q: **Why did the vampire forget his cape at home?**

A: Because he was going batty.

Q: **What do you get when you combine a bear and a ghost?**

A: Winnie the Boo

Knock, knock.

Who's there?

Candy.

Candy who?

Candy be time for Halloween already?

Q: **What is a turkey's favorite dessert?**

A: Apple gobbler

Q: **Where does Dracula go when he visits New York City?**

A: The Vampire State Building

Q: **What does a zombie call a race car driver?**

A: Fast food

Q: **What does a cow like to dress up as for Halloween?**

A: A mooo-vie star

Q: **Why can't you invite an optometrist to your Halloween party?**

A: Because she'll make a spectacle of herself.

Q: **What do you get when you cross a monkey and a ghost?**

A: A ba-boo-n

Q: **Where did the werewolf keep his coat?**

A: In his claw-set

Q: **Why don't clumsy people like autumn?**

A: They're afraid they'll fall.

Knock, knock.

Who's there?

Dubai.

Dubai who?

We need Dubai some more Halloween candy.

Knock, knock.

Who's there?

Muffin.

Muffin who?

Muffin is going to stop me from trick-or-treating this year.

Q: Why are bats so lazy?

A: Because they just hang around all the time.

Q: What is a monster's favorite musical?

A: *Phantom of the Opera*

Knock, knock.

Who's there?

Avery.

Avery who?

Avery Happy Halloween to everybody!

Knock, knock.

Who's there?

Berry.

Berry who?

I'm berry glad that fall is here.

- -

Q: What do vampires do with their buddies?

A: They fang out!

Q: What kind of coffee does a wizard like?

A: Dark brew

**Q: What happened when the vampires had
a race?**

A: They were neck and neck the whole time.

Knock, knock.

Who's there?

Otter.

Otter who?

**You otter carve your pumpkin
before Halloween.**

Knock, knock.

Who's there?

Bat.

Bat who?

I bat you're going to open the door on Halloween.

Q: What did the werewolf do after he was told a joke?

A: He howled with laughter.

Q: Why wouldn't you want to make a witch mad?

A: Because they're always flying off the handle.

Knock, knock.

Who's there?

Moe.

Moe who?

I want Moe Halloween candy!

Knock, knock.

Who's there?

Weird.

Weird who?

Weird all my Halloween candy go?

Knock, knock.

Who's there?

Police.

Police who?

Police come to my Halloween party!

**Q: What does the caretaker think of
the cemetery?**

A: He really digs it!

Q: What is Dracula's favorite kind of soup?

A: Alpha-bat soup

Knock, knock.

Who's there?

Juicy.

Juicy who?

Did juicy my new Halloween costume?

Knock, knock.

Who's there?

Orange.

Orange who?

Orange you glad it's Halloween?

Knock, knock.

Who's there?

Howl.

Howl who?

Howl I get my Halloween candy if you don't open the door?

Q: What do you get when you cross a werewolf and a forest?

A: A fur tree

Knock, knock.

Who's there?

Latte.

Latte who?

It's a latte fun going trick-or-treating with you.

Q: What's a black cat's favorite dessert?

A: Mice cream

Knock, knock.

Who's there?

Candice.

Candice who?

Candice Halloween party be any more fun?

Knock, knock.

Who's there?

Oswald.

Oswald who?

Oswald my Halloween candy and it got stuck in my throat!

- -

Q: Why did Frankenstein stop going to the gym?

A: Because it wasn't working out.

Q: How did the zombie write a book?

A: He hired a ghost writer.

Q: What is a ghost's favorite amusement park ride?

A: The scary-go-round

Q: What kind of cheese did the goblin put on his pizza?

A: Munster cheese

Q: What do ghosts do in their spare time?

A: They read boo-ks.

Q: Why did Dracula get tricked out of his lollipops?

A: Because he's a sucker.

Q: What is a monster's favorite dinner dish?

A: Fettuccine Afraid-o

Q: When do ghosts like to go for walks?

A: Sometime in the moaning

Q: What's black, white, and red all over?

A: Dracula with a sunburn

Q: **What do you get when a dentist cleans a zombie's teeth?**

A: A brush with death

Q: **How do zombies like their steak?**

A: Very, very rare

Q: **What do you call a black cat that has eight legs and likes to swim?**

A: An octo-puss

Q: **What did the zombie say when it looked in my closet?**

A: "I wouldn't be caught dead in these clothes!"

- -

Q: What kind of monster is always alert?

A: An aware-wolf

Q: What kind of parties do monsters like to go to?

A: Ma-scare-ade parties

Knock, knock.

Who's there?

Andy.

Andy who?

Andy-body want to go to the costume party with me?

Q: Why did Jimmy bury his flashlight in the cemetery?

A: The batteries were dead.

Q: Why can't a monster eat more than three dentists?

A: Because they're so filling.

Q: Why are pilgrims so popular?

A: Because Plymouth rocks!

Jimmy: How long does it take to read a ghost story?

Johnny: Not long if you book it.

Q: Why was the road so mad at the trick-or-treaters?

A: They kept crossing it.

- -

Q: Why can't you trust the swamp monster?

A: There's something fishy about him.

Q: What do you get if you throw four zombies in a lake?

A: Cuatro sinko

Q: How do you choose which Halloween candy to buy?

A: It takes a lot of cents.

Q: Why wouldn't the monster eat the clown?

A: He tasted funny.

Jimmy: Your banana costume is ugly!

Johnny: That hurt my peelings!

Q: How did the farmer fix his overalls?

A: With a pumpkin patch

Q: Why couldn't the kid ring the doorbell when he was trick-or-treating?

A: He was a ding-dong.

Q: How did Dracula fix his broken fangs?

A: With tooth-paste

Q: How can I learn more about poisonous spiders?

A: Look it up on a web-site.

Q: Why do we bob for apples on Halloween?

A: Because watermelons are too heavy.

Q: What happened to the chef when he forgot the yams?

A: He got canned.

Q: What kind of flowers bloom on Halloween?

A: Chrysanthe-mums

Jill: I stitched up the hole in your Halloween costume.

Jane: Well, I'll be darned.

Q: Did you hear about the monster who was hit by lightning?

A: It was shocking.

Susie: I think I'll dress up like a lightbulb for Halloween.

Stacy: That's a bright idea!

Q: Why was the witch late for school?

A: Her broom over-swept.

Q: What's a zombie's favorite painting?

A: *The Moan-a Lisa*

Q: What did Godzilla eat for breakfast?

A: A chew-chew train

Joe: Did you find the missing apples from the orchard?

Sam: No. My search was fruitless.

Q: Why is Frankenstein so good at gardening?

A: He has a green thumb.

Mother: We're having your aunt and uncle for Thanksgiving.

Daughter: I was hoping we were having turkey and stuffing.

Q: Why should you dress up as King Arthur for Halloween?

A: You'll be sure to have a good knight.

Q: What runs around a cemetery but never moves?

A: A fence

Q: What do you call a black cat that carries your wallet and keys?

A: A purrrrrse

Q: Why can't you take pigs trick-or-treating?

A: They'll hog all the candy.

Q: **What do you call a witch whose broom won't fly?**

A: You call a cab.

Q: **What is a zombie's favorite game?**

A: Swallow the Leader

Q: **Why was the pilgrim embarrassed?**

A: Because he saw the turkey dressing.

Q: **What do you call a witch's lost geometry book?**

A: Hex-a-gone

Q: **How do you keep monsters out of your closet?**

A: Put them under the bed.

Knock, knock.

Who's there?

Harry.

Harry who?

Harry up. It's time to carve our pumpkins!

Joey: Are you charging your flashlight for Halloween?

Jenny: No. I'm paying cash for it.

Q: **What happened after the black cats had a fight?**

A: They hissed and made up.

Q: Why are werewolves so competitive?

A: It's a dog-eat-dog world out there.

Q: How did the witch stay dry without an umbrella?

A: It wasn't raining.

Q: What do you call a scary dream about a horse?

A: A night-mare

Q: Where do witches buy their pets?

A: From a black cat-alog

Knock, knock.

Who's there?

Luke.

Luke who?

Luke at all the candy I got for Halloween!

Q: Why did the pie crust go to the dentist?

A: Because it needed a filling.

Q: What happens when a monster shows up in the barnyard?

A: It's udder chaos.

Q: What is the silliest Halloween candy?

A: Candy corn-y

Q: What do black cats have that no other animals have?

A: Kittens

Q: What do you get when you cross a skeleton and a trumpet?

A: A trom-bone

Q: Did you hear the story about the giant?

A: It was a tall tale.

Q: What do you get when you cross a werewolf and a clock?

A: A watchdog

Q: What do you give a monster for Halloween?

A: Whatever he wants!

Q: How do you make a pineapple shake?

A: You tell it a ghost story!

Q: Where do horses go trick-or-treating?

A: All over the neigh-borhood

Betty: I'm wearing a Mona Lisa costume

for Halloween.

Bailey: You'll be pretty as a picture.

Q: What does a zombie call a black belt?

A: Kung-food

Q: What does a bat do for fun?

A: Hangs out with its friends

Q: Why did the witch take a nap?

A: She was hex-austed.

Joe: Why did you put ketchup on your pumpkin pie?

John: Because we're all out of mustard.

Ella: Is that a real photo of Bigfoot hanging on your wall?

Anna: No, it's an im-poster.

Q: How does a ghost stay out of trouble?

A: It stays on its best boo-havior.

Henry: Do zombies like sausage for breakfast?

Harry: No, they think it's the wurst.

Q: Why didn't Dracula sharpen his fangs?

A: He thought it was pointless.

Q: How do you wake up a chicken for Thanksgiving?

A: With an alarm cluck.

Q: Why can't ghosts fool anyone?

A: You can see right through them.

Q: What do you call a photo of a vampire's fangs?

A: A tooth pic

- -

Q: Why did the farmer plant his phone in the garden?

A: He wanted to grow a call-iflower.

Q: Why did the preschoolers have to go to jail the day after Halloween?

A: They were kid-napping.

Q: Why did the farmer drop his tools on the ground?

A: He wanted to have a hoe-down.

Pete: Would a monster eat your math teacher?

Paul: You can count on it.

Q: **What do you get when you cross a mouse and a campfire on Halloween?**

A: A cheesy ghost story

Q: **Why did the witch put a frog in her drink?**

A: She wanted some croak-a-cola.

Q: **Who likes to sing about their Halloween candy?**

A: Candy rappers

Q: **Why couldn't Jimmy find a detective costume for Halloween?**

A: He was clueless.

Q: Why did the farmer want to be president?

A: So he could work for world peas.

Knock, knock.

Who's there?

Ears.

Ears who?

Ears a few more good Halloween jokes for you.

Q: What do you call a safe driver on Halloween?

A: Wreck-less

Q: What do you call a zombie who's lost his eyeballs?

A: Unsightly

Q: **Why did the zombie dislike the farmers' market?**

A: Because there were no farmers for sale.

Q: **Why did the werewolf need a flea collar?**

A: It was itching to howl at the moon.

Q: **What do you get when you cross a dinosaur, a basset hound, and gorilla?**

A: Dog-zilla

Q: **Why don't rabbits like spooky stories?**

A: Because it makes the hare stand up on the backs of their necks.

Q: If April showers bring May flowers, what do May flowers bring?

A: Pilgrims.

Q: What do you get when you cross Dracula and a cell phone?

A: A bat-mobile

Q: What is a turkey's favorite dessert?

A: Cherry gobbler

Q: What is a ghost's favorite movie?

A: *Goon with the Wind*

- -

Knock, knock.

Who's there?

Weed.

Weed who?

Weed better go trick-or-treating soon.

Knock, knock.

Who's there?

Dozen.

Dozen who?

Dozen anyone ever open their door on

Halloween anymore?

Knock, knock.

Who's there?

Wade.

Wade who?

Wade a minute—I want to go trick-or-treating too!

Q: What kind of mail do famous werewolves get?

A: Fang mail

Q: What is a witch's favorite cereal?

A: C-hex

Q: What is a pumpkin's least favorite sport?

A: Squash

Knock, knock.

Who's there?

Fitness.

Fitness who?

I'm fitness whole pumpkin pie in my mouth!

Knock, knock.

Who's there?

Wool.

Wool who?

Wool you go trick-or-treating with me?

Q: What is a werewolf's favorite holiday?

A: Fangs-giving

Q: Why did the turkey decide to play the drums?

A: Because he already had the drumsticks.

Q: What did the vet give the sick black cat?

A: A purr-scription

Knock, knock.

Who's there?

Sherwood.

Sherwood who?

Sherwood be nice if you'd come to the

Halloween party with me.

Josh: Did you hear the joke about the skeleton?

Jeff: No, I haven't.

Josh: That's too bad—it's pretty humerus.

Q: Why did the vampire visit the library?

A: He was looking for a good book to sink his

teeth into!

- -

Knock, knock.

Who's there?

Window.

Window who?

Window we go trick-or-treating?

Q: Why isn't Dracula's nose 12 inches long?

A: Because then it would be a foot.

Q: Why did the turkey strike out at the ball game?

A: He kept hitting fowl balls.

Q: What do pumpkins wear for Halloween?

A: A har-vest

Sammy: Why are you slicing up all the dinner rolls?

Stuart: Because the doctor told me to cut my carbs.

Knock, knock.

Who's there?

Turkey.

Turkey who?

No, turkeys say "gobble, gobble." Owls say "who."

Knock, knock.

Who's there?

Cauliflower.

Cauliflower who?

Cauliflower doesn't have a last name.

- -

Q: How do you know when a turkey is on the line?

A: You'll hear the phone go *wing, wing.*

Knock, knock.

Who's there?

Mustache.

Mustache who?

I mustache you if you want to go trick-or-treating.

Q: What country do monsters come from?

A: The imagi-nation

Q: What do you get when you cross a witch with a wasp?

A: A spell-ing bee

Q: What do zombies like to eat for dinner?

A: Tomb-stone pizzas

Knock, knock.

Who's there?

Lava.

Lava who?

I lava the leaves in autumn!

Knock, knock.

Who's there?

Kenya.

Kenya who?

Kenya come to the Halloween party?

Q: What do ghosts do when they can't get their computer to work?

A: They re-boo-t it.

Knock, knock.

Who's there?

Woo.

Woo who?

You seem pretty excited about Halloween!

Q: How do you find a zombie's house?

A: Look for a dead-end street.

Knock, knock.

Who's there?

Owen.

Owen who?

You Owen me some more Halloween candy!

Q: **What do you get if you wear antlers with your pirate costume?**

A: A buck-aneer

Q: **Why does Humpty Dumpty like autumn so much?**

A: Because he always has a great fall!

Q: **Why did the vampire stop working?**

A: Because he was on his coffin break.

Q: **Why did the turkey have to go to the principal's office?**

A: Because it was using fowl language.

- -

Q: How do you know that someone has eaten too much on Thanksgiving?

A: Because they're thank-full.

Knock, knock.

Who's there?

Canoe.

Canoe who?

Canoe come over for Thanksgiving?

Knock, knock.

Who's there?

Yugo.

Yugo who?

Yugo trick-or-treat first, and I'll go second.

Knock, knock.

Who's there?

Howard.

Howard who?

Howard I know? He's wearing a Halloween costume!

Knock, knock.

Who's there?

Dora.

Dora who?

The Dora's locked on Halloween? That's crazy!

Q: Why did the girl put her Halloween candy under her pillow?

A: Because she wanted to have sweet dreams.

Knock, knock.

Who's there?

Juneau.

Juneau who?

Juneau, I think it's going to be a really great Halloween!

Knock, knock.

Who's there?

Gladys.

Gladys who?

I'm Gladys Halloween, because I love candy!

Q: What did the sweet potato say to the turkey?

A: "I yam what I yam!"

Knock, knock.

Who's there?

Cheryl.

Cheryl who?

I'm Cheryl get a lot of Halloween candy this year.

Q: What's blue and has feathers?

A: A turkey holding its breath

Q: What happens when you forget to put your turkey in the refrigerator?

A: It becomes fowl.

Q: What kind of key has feathers but can't open doors?

A: Tur-keys

Q: **What do scarecrows and turkeys have in common?**

A: They both get filled with stuffing.

Josh: Does Dracula like wearing plaid?

Jeff: I don't know, but I'll check.

Leah: Do you like corn for Thanksgiving?

Anna: It's a-maize-ing.

Q: **When is a turkey funny?**

A: When it's being a ham.

Knock, knock.

Who's there?

Witch.

Witch who?

I want to witch you a very Happy Halloween!

Q: Why didn't the mummy answer the phone?

A: Because he was tied up at the time.

Q: What's a werewolf's favorite time of year?

A: Howl-oween

Q: What did the goblin say to the skeleton?

A: "I've got a bone to pick with you!"

Q: Where do ghosts go to get training?

A: Boo-t camp

Knock, knock.

> Who's there?

Who?

> Who who?

Wouldn't you like to know!

Q: What did the leaf say to the tree?

A: I'm falling for you.

Knock, knock.

> Who's there?

Twix.

> Twix who?

Twix or treat.

Knock, knock.

Who's there?

Italy.

Italy who?

Italy a shame if you can't go trick-or-treating with us.

Knock, knock.

Who's there?

Darren.

Darren who?

I'm Darren you to wear a chicken costume for Halloween!

Knock, knock.

Who's there?

Owl.

Owl who?

Owl give you some of my Halloween candy if you open the door!

Knock, knock.

Who's there?

Donut.

Donut who?

Donut worry, be happy—it's Halloween!

Knock, knock.

Who's there?

Europe.

Europe who?

Europe to no good this Halloween, aren't you?

- -

Knock, knock.

> Who's there?

Gas.

> Gas who?

Gas who has a great collection of Halloween jokes.

Q: What's a goblin's favorite food?

A: Ghoul-ash

Q: Why did the turkey want everyone to stay out of the kitchen?

A: Because it was dressing!

Q: How do pilgrims bake their pumpkin pies?

A: With May-flour

Q: What's it like to ride a witch's broom?

A: It's terri-flying.

Billy: You'll never be a pumpkin farmer.

Joey: Stop squashing my dreams!

Knock, knock.

Who's there?

Arthur.

Arthur who?

Arthur any leftovers from Thanksgiving dinner?

Knock, knock.

Who's there?

Idaho.

Idaho who?

Idaho the pumpkin patch, but I'm too busy trick-or-treating!

Knock, knock.

Who's there?

Lion.

Lion who?

I'd be lion if I said I didn't love Halloween!

Q: What do you get when you cross a zombie and a donut?

A: A hole-y terror

Q: What part of a turkey smells the best?

A: Its nose!

Q: What happens if you get sick on Halloween?

A: You get a fever and chills.

Q: What do you get when you cross a skeleton, a cyclops, and a piece of meat?

A: A rib-eye steak

Janie: How does that ghost look so young?

Jessie: It uses Boo-tox.

Q: When is it funny to be a farmer?

A: During the har-har-harvest

Q: What do you call a monster who's afraid of trick-or-treaters?

A: A Hallo-weenie

Q: What's an undertaker's favorite drink?

A: Cran-bury juice

Q: When is a turkey afraid to cross the road?

A: When he's a chicken.

Mom: Where are we going to put all the Thanksgiving leftovers?

Grandma: We'll cross that fridge when we come to it.

Q: Why do cyclopses get along so well?

A: They always see eye to eye.

Q: How often do you see a ghost?

A: Once in a boo moon

Q: What do you call it when a trick-or-treater gives you all his candy?

A: A blessing in disguise

Q: Why don't zombies eat elephants?

A: They don't want to bite off more than they can chew.

- -

Q: What do scarecrows do when they're tired?

A: They hit the hay.

Stanley: Are you afraid of skeletons?

Henry: There's no bones about it.

Q: Why wouldn't Jimmy carve a pumpkin

for Halloween?

A: He was out of his gourd.

Q: Why did the monster turn into a human?

A: Because you are what you eat.

Q: Who's the most fun at a Halloween party?

A: The owls—they're a hoot!

Q: Why can't you tell if it's a real ghost or a Halloween costume?

A: Because you can't judge a spook by its cover.

Q: How does everybody like the new cemetery?

A: It got grave reviews.

Knock, knock.

Who's there?

Radio.

Radio who?

Radio not, I'm going trick-or-treating!

Knock, knock.

Who's there?

Uganda.

Uganda who?

Uganda go trick-or-treating with me?

Knock, knock.

Who's there?

Jester.

Jester who?

Jester minute, I want to go to the Halloween party too!

Knock, knock.

Who's there?

Ketchup.

Ketchup who?

You better ketchup if you want to go trick-or-treating.

Q: How do you catch a ghost?

A: With a boo-by trap

Q: What do farmers say when they play poker?

A: "Weed 'em and reap!"

Betsy: What do you think of my egg costume?

Bailey: It cracks me up!

Q: Where do you put a crazy scarecrow?

A: In the funny farm

Q: What happened when the undertaker got a cramp in his leg?

A: He got a charley hearse.

Terry: Will zombies chew on your head?

Tommy: That's a no-brainer.

Q: What do you get when you cross a pig and a unicorn?

A: Pig-asus!

Q: What do you get when you cross Bigfoot and a pumpkin?

A: Sa-squash

- -

Knock, knock.

Who's there?

Dragon.

Dragon who?

I'm tired of dragon this huge bag of

Halloween candy.

Q: What do you get if you trick-or-treat at the

train station?

A: Choo-choo-ing gum

Q: What happens if you lose track of time

on Halloween?

A: You'll be choco-late for trick-or-treating!

- -

Tongue Twisters—Say each one ten times fast!

Twisted turkey toes

Crunchy coated candy corn

Twitchy witches

Gross ghosts

Rare scarecrow

Knock, knock.

Who's there?

Oliver.

Oliver who?

I'm really sad this joke book is Oliver!